MERRY CHRISTMAS Samantha Reindeer

By
Eugene Bradley Coco
Illustrated by
Lisa Haughom

Incorporated

Copyright © 1993 by Kidsbooks, Inc.
3535 West Peterson Avenue
Chicago, IL 60659

Printed in Canada
Hardcover editions bound in the United States of America

It was Christmas Eve, and everyone at the North Pole was helping Santa get ready for his midnight ride. The elves were busy in Santa's workshop, wrapping presents and loading them onto Santa's sleigh.

Mrs. Claus was putting the finishing touches on Santa's new snowsuit. And outside, Santa's reindeer were lining up for their final instructions of the night.

"Now remember to keep your eyes open and your heads up," warned Santa. "And don't forget to watch out for birds and airplanes."

Just then, Santa felt a tug at his leg. It was Samantha Reindeer.

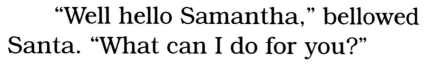

"Well hello Samantha," bellowed
Santa. "What can I do for you?"
"I was wondering if I could help pull
your sleigh tonight," she asked.
"You're too small to pull a sleigh
with us," laughed the other reindeer.

"Don't listen to them," said Santa, as he knelt down beside Samantha. "Not too long ago, they were just as small as you. Next year, when you've grown a bit, you can help pull my sleigh."

"But I'm big enough now," sobbed Samantha. "Besides, next year is so far away. Can't I help you tonight?"

"I'm sorry, Samantha," said Santa, "but I already have enough reindeer to help me. Now, I have to get going. It's late."

Santa climbed into his sleigh and let out a great big "Ho! Ho! Ho!" Off he flew, with all of the presents, into the snowy sky.

As Samantha watched Santa fly over the trees, she saw one of the presents fall to the ground. She called out to Santa, but he didn't hear her.

"This is terrible," said Samantha, as she read the name on the present. "If I don't do something, Lauren won't get her Christmas present."

First, Samantha went over to Santa's house for help, but Mrs. Claus was sound asleep. Then, she peeked inside Santa's workshop, but all of the elves were sleeping, too.

"What am I going to do now?" sighed Samantha. "It's almost Christmas."

"Why don't you just deliver the present yourself," said Thomas Elf, as he opened the workshop door.

"What are you doing up so late?" asked Samantha. "Aren't you tired from wrapping all the Christmas presents?"

"The other elves wouldn't let me help them," said Thomas. "They said that I was too small."

"That's what the big reindeer told me when I asked to fly with Santa," said Samantha. "But we'll show them. We're not too small. We'll deliver Lauren's present ourselves, just like you said."

Thomas was very excited. "Ready when you are!" he cried, as he pulled his hat down over his ears and tied his scarf on extra tight.

"There's just one problem," sighed Samantha.

"What's that?" asked Thomas.

"I'm scared," said Samantha. "I've never flown outside the North Pole before."

"Don't worry," said Thomas, "I'll watch out for you. I'll make sure everything is alright."

"Okay," agreed Samantha.

Thomas picked up Lauren's present, hopped on Samantha's back, and held on with all of his might.

"Here we go!" called Samantha.

She took a deep breath and started running as fast as she could. The next thing Samantha knew, she was gliding past Santa's workshop, over the trees, and through the clouds.

"I did it! I did it!" cried Samantha, as she looked down at all the houses sparkling with Christmas lights. "I made it beyond the North Pole!"

After a while, Samantha and Thomas found Lauren's house. As quietly as she could, Samantha landed on the roof and tiptoed over to Lauren's window.

Lauren was fast asleep, dreaming of Santa Claus and Christmas presents, when suddenly she heard a **THUMP**. "What was that noise?" she said, as she turned on the light and rolled out of bed.

Lauren couldn't believe her eyes when she looked outside and saw Samantha and Thomas peering in.

"It's a real live reindeer!" she cried. "And a cute little elf, too!"

Lauren opened her window, and Samantha and Thomas came inside.

"We're delivering your Christmas gift," said Samantha. "I hope you don't mind."

"Of course not," said Lauren, as she gave Samantha and Thomas some Christmas cookies and milk. "Meeting you is the best Christmas present that I could ever get."

"We better be going," said Thomas. "We have a long trip home."

"Be careful," said Lauren, as she hugged them both. "Merry Christmas!"

It was morning when Samantha and Thomas made it back to the North Pole.

"It's so quiet," said Thomas. "Where could everyone be?"

"They're probably cleaning up Santa's workshop and getting ready for next year," said Samantha.

But when Samantha opened the workshop door, the elves weren't working. They were waiting for her. And so were the other reindeer, along with Santa Claus himself!

"Merry Christmas, Samantha Reindeer!" bellowed Santa, as everyone let out a great big cheer.
"I'm so proud of you. If it wasn't for you, Lauren
would never have gotten her present this
Christmas."

"I couldn't have done it without Thomas," said Samantha. "But how did you know about Lauren's present?" she asked.

"Santa knows everything," said Mrs. Claus, as she winked at Santa.

Samantha could hardly keep her eyes open as all the other reindeer gathered around to congratulate her.

"It's time you went to sleep," said Santa as he picked up Samantha and carried her to bed. "You've had a very busy night."

But Samantha didn't hear Santa. She was already fast asleep, dreaming of all the presents she would deliver next Christmas Eve.